CURSE OF THE MYSTICAL ISLAND

PIYUSH GOTEKAR

I dedicate this book to my loving parents:

Mr.Pundlik Gotekar

and

Mrs.Pratima Gotekar

Contents

Preface

I started writing this book a few months before in my school.I got the idea of writing through some of my freinds.I am not much experienced for this and yes,its my first time.So,there may be mistakes in it.Please forgive me for those and enjoy it as much you can.

Acknowledgements

My first debt is to Notionpress Publication itself for helping me to publish my first book ever.Then I would like to acknowledge my classmates and freinds whose names I've used in my book.Abhay D.,Himanshu W.,Jeet F.,Krupesh C.,Nayan M.,Prajwal T.,Prathamesh V.,Chhavya N.,Dipanshu B.,Gaurav P.,Prashik D.,Sahil S.,Rohit K.,Aman W.,Aditya L.,Sahil W.,Raj R.,Shivam S.,Alhaj S.,Aditya K.,Kamal T.,Harshal D.,Bhargav H.,Atharva Kadu.,Kunal S.,Ashmit B.,Aniket M.,Kausthubh W.,Debank J.,Manav K.,VedantS.,Pratyush B.,Pratik P.,Rohan,Lankesh K.,Purvesh G.,Lokesh S. and Romaditya D.

Special thanks to my freind Pruthviraj Shid for helping me while writing the story.And, thanks to Vinay for helping me start writing along with Parth Wankhede,Yatharth Dhanvij and Aryan Dhanke.

1

Goal!

So....I...can.....do....it.I said to myself wheezing.My mind was shaking.Screams along with cheers were echoing from all 4 sides.I-I was breathing very heavily. I got a step back, one more step back, and got myself the suitable distance that I wanted. Sweat was dropping slowly passing my right cheek. I took long breath, starting with a short walk, I ran towards the ball and kicked it towards the goalpost with as much strength as possible. It flew towards the goalpost piercing the air blocking its way, directly into the left-bottom corner. Everyone in their there started screaming," "Goal!!!!" I couldn't bear the happiness and got down on my knees. All of my team-mates came and grabbed me and started Screaming with joy. "So here, Center Point School wins the match by 5-6" said the anchors over the loudspeaker. I couldn't believe my eyes nor my ears. I was still unable to explain my emotions. Whatever they were, I was very, very happy.

Me and my team was called the up the stage for prize ceremony. While everyone was awarded with a gold medal,I was also given the title for the most goals in the match. Yeah, I do am a good player, but you know, when everyone is dependent on you, it doesn't matter how talented or skillful are, your self confidence just slides down. whatever, it doesn't mattered me. I won, my team won, my school won, done! Nothing else we got down the stage while I was praising myself in my own world. Others were been given consolation prizes but I didn't cared.

After around more 15 mins, the prize ceremony finished along with it was my wait. Finally, the time to go back home. And also, get some refreshments! My most favourite thing whenever I go to an interschool competition,I win or lose, what I love the most are refreshments. "Children, get near the bus till I get y'all some refreshments."said Kunal sir. He was our coach. "Yes Sir!" we replied in an echoe.

All of our boys marched towards the bus which would be taking us back to school. "The last goal was literally marvelous!How you just did it Aditya?" admired Sahil. "Just did it. I can't really explain the moment."I replied."I wish that I could play like you." continued Sahil. I was in my thoughts until I realised that we were lagging behind and everyone was a bit far ahead of us both.We increased our pace to cope-up with others.

As we reached near the bus, we were able to see Kunal sir at a distance. My eyes were bursting out seeing him with many big boxes in his hands. His every step made me more eagerly wait for those snacks. In my mind as I closed my eyes, I could see Samosa, Kachori, Dosa, Idli, Chole Bhature, Vada, Omelet, Gulab Jamun, Fried rice,Kofta, Pakoda, Sandwich, Pizza, Burger, Cold Drink, as I kept on thinking, a strong voice broke my beautiful, sweet dream,"Come on boys, everyone pickup one box and get inside." ordered Kunal Sir along with the boxes in his hands. My excitement was at its peak. Yes,I do am a foodie guy and I can't live without being so.Everyone took a single box and entered the bus. I walked towards him, took a box and entered the bus.I moved my eyes around in search of a window seat. The 4th seat on the left side was empty. I slowly walked towards it while suddenly someone slipped through and lied down on the seat.

"Abhay, stand up!" I shouted. He was a bit like round, had a cute face, but he loved to trouble others. "And if I say -no, then?" said Abhay. "Please bro, get up,I chose this seat first. I am in a nice mood and I literally, don't want to down it."I requested. He was a nice guy, but sometimes bullied others. "Ok, just for once."he agreed. He stood up and started moving while I got down on my desired seat. I sat down slowly and opened the window. I got the box and opened it. I could see 1 samosa, 1 sandwich, 1 pack of lassi,and 2 sweets."Everyone in ?"asked Kunal sir. "Yes everyone is here sir!" said Manav. He was our team captain and Kunal sir trusted him a lot.

Finally the engine started and bus moved."Let's play a game." suggested Chhavya."nice idea,but which game" asked Dipanshu. "No games, let's sing songs." said Manav and everyone agreed. He was a very nice guy and no one disagreed him. Everyone started singing carols but I was just busy eating.

Our bus travelled bit long.It was around 5:15 PM when we reached our school and I was really-really very tired. I just got my cycle and rode to home.As I was riding, I could see some people gathered on road. It seemed like a case of an accident. Suddenly,I heard an ambulance coming from my behind. I didn't paid much attention and rode back to home.

2

Ding-Dong!

It took around 15 mins for me to reach my home. "I'm back!" I said as I entered inside. "How was the match ?" asked Shivam. my brother, li'l brother. "Just nailed it!" I Said cheerfully. "Where's mom n' dad?" I asked. "Mom has been to market while dad's in the basement". "OK,I'll wash my face and tell him about the match." I moved through the corridor, passed the guest room and reached the washroom.

I washed my face and was feeling very tired. It was evening.I got my towel and rubbed my face while walking down towards the basement.I opened the door quietly and was able to see stairs going deep down in the dark. I stepped down slowly piercing the silence while I could just hear out my footsteps clearly.It was very dark down there as the lights were broken since a week.I don't know why, but I was feeling a bit uneasy even while going through the same, familiar path. As I was walking down, suddenly, my foot slipped and I fell down. I couldn't control myself and ended up crashing to a wall.

I stood up, it was very dark down there. I wasn't feeling familiar with the place anymore. I wasn't just able to understand what was happening with me. I couldn't see anything there. I screamed,"Is anyone out there? Dad?" I was getting to feel a bit scared while suddenly, a hand got placed on my shoulder and I cried,"Aaaaaaaaaahhhhhhhhhhhh!!!!!!!!","what happened!Why're you screaming?" asked my Mom in a bit like strong voice. I woke up with a shock."Was it just a dream? Thank God!" I sighed. It was just kinda a... beautiful nightmare. "Now stop dreaming and get ready for school. Also, call for your little brother, he must be sleeping" said my mom. "Ok, I'll do it." I said while yawning. My mom stepped out of the room but I was still thinking about the nightmare. It just hit a bit different.

I slowly got down the bed, still yawning and first of all, got a glimpse of myself in the minor just beside my bed, "Why I am so handsome!" I praised myself which was like a daily routine. I went downstairs to my brother's room to wake him up as I was ordered.Walking and walking slowly towards his room while my dream was still revolving in my mind.I push opened the door upon reaching there and stepped inside, "Shivu, wake up!" I said cudling him. "What happened?Who are you?" he said being half asleep. "Who are you?Wake up fast and get ready for school!" It tried to scold him. "What the hell is this school,why the fridge does it exists !" He continued. It was usual for him to act like a drunk every morning. "Stop making excuses and get ready fast!", "Ok-ok give me 5 mins."he replied.I Came out and headed towards the washroom.

As I got towards it, accidently, my eyes fell upon the calendar, hanged on the left side of washroom. I checked the date 6 March 2022 and literally I was surprised in happiness to see it was a Sunday.Mom!It's Sunday today!Hence no school!" I screamed in joy, but Mom didn't paid attention and was distracted by the doorbell which rang just a second before.

Soon I could hear my mom calling out,"Aditya! Come fast here!", "What happened?" I asked but she interrupted. "Don't utter a single word,just come here running."I followed the order and ran towards the door.As soon as I reached there, I saw mom holding a big envelope in her hands. "What's this?" I asked. "Try checking yourself." replied my mom handing over the envelope to me.The envelope read as,

"To.
Mr. Romaditya,
House no. 4, Aman nagar,
Nagpur

"This is our address and it belongs to dad but, wait a min,who brought it here?" I asked mom " I-I don't know that how it came up here. I just heard the doorbell and opened the door. I couldn't see the person who rang the bell but the only thing visible was this envelope. Try out opening it" she said.

As I was about to tear open it,I saw dad coming from the front corridor. "What's that?" he asked seeing the envelope in my hand. "Its for you only." I replied. He came nearer and taking the envelope in his hands, started looking towards it with curiosity. Everyone was eagerly waiting for the envelope to open. He cleverly tear opened the envelope and took out a letter like something. He started reading,

"From,
Alhaj Tour Agency,
Mumbai
Date:05-03-2022
To,
Mr. Romaditya
House no. 4,Aman Nagar,

Nagpur

Sub: Prize courier

Respected Sir,

I am Pratyush,from Alhaj Tour Agency and I am writing this to you to inform you about a lucky draw.As you must be knowing that about a month ago,we had a scheme of a lucky draw in which 10 families would be selected for a free tour to Hawai.All those who purchased a family package were eligible for the draw along with your family.

As per your fate,your family has got selected for the tour along with 9 other.We are sending your plane tickets,hotel details and other information with this letter.It'll be great for you to know that you all are going to get free lodging,food and travel facilities.Enjoy your tour and promote us too.Till then,

Bon Voyage.

Thanking you

Pratyush

Mail us at:Alhajtouragency420@gmail.com"

"Is it a joke?" asked mom eyerolling . "I-I don't think so." said dad holding the plane tickets in his hands."Means we are re-really going to Hawai?" I said being amazingly dumbstruck.We all just couldn't bear our emotions and started dancing in joy.As we were dancing,Shivam came and was a bit like shocked seeing us in such a state.He asked,"What happened?Did a dancing snake bit you all?" We first laughed at his dumb face and then explained him the scene.

"But,what's the date of the flight?" asked mom.Dad checked the tickets and said being a bit tensed,"It says that we need to depart on the day after tommorow.We need to get ready fast.","We'll not get such a chance once more.We mustn't leave it."said mom.

It was afternoon and we were busy doing our packing. I kept on thinking all the things need to be packed- clothes, stationery, lock, toothbrush, toothpaste, goggles, camera, bottles, first aid kit, etc. As I was searching for the items, mom asked dad,"Everything's fine, but what about the passports?" , "Don't you remember? We made them for our trip to Thailand." replied dad."But I don't remember such an incident." said mom being confused. "Let it be, don't worry. " said dad.

It was around 5:00PM when we were almost done with packing.Sitting on a couch, I decided to go and meet my freinds. " Mom I'll be back in half n' hour " I said. "Ok! Try to return before dinner."I could hear her say from the kitchen.I got out of the house and strode along the road towards the park where usually my freinds would get gathered. As soon as reached their, they recognized me and I was able to hear, Hey Aditya!Where're you going?"

I got out of the house and strode along the road towards the park where usually. my freinds would get gathered. As soon as reached their, they recognized me and I was able to hear, Hey Adityal where're you going?"

"Nowhere, just wanted to meet y'all only.I do have something amazing to tell you all.", "Come here and tell fast then. "continued Ashmit. "Yes, but where's Prashik?" I asked."No idea! We went to call for him but-" "But his house was locked and his phone was also showing out of network." interrupted Kamal.Prashik was a nice freind of mine and I loved to share many of my things with him. "OK, fine,but I wish he could also hear this. "I desired. "But atleast tell us now that what's the thing?" said Vedant. "Ok, so listen, what just happened is that around a month ago, we had participated in a lucky draw and...","and...?" Vedant interrupted me." And luckily we got selected !" I continued

"Wow what a nice joke!" taunted Debank."It's not a joke.We really do won."I tried to explain.

"Ok,but what did you won, a cooker?" asked Ashmit, "I know that you all won't believe my words but still I'll love to tell y'all. So what I won is... a free tour to Hawaii" I told very excitedly "Really?" asked Debank. His face clearly said that he had a doubt on my statement."You need to believe me. Its the truth and I'm just departing the day after tommorow" I explained. "I think we can believe him.He may be true." Ashmit said to the other both and they too agreed.

3

Something's Weird

We had a nice talk while I bent my head down and saw the time 6:47 PM in my watch."I think I should get going."I said to them."Ok then,lets leave.Bye,see you later."said Debank ."Bye." I replied and headed towards my home and was feeling a bit hungry.As I walked down the market,I felt like being in another world as I could smell the aroma in my surrounding coming from the shops, restaurants and street vendors in there. Still, I tried to control myself and continued my journey back to home.

I reached home back at around 6:50 PM and could still see everyone busy working. Mom was busy cooking food in the kitchen while dad seemed to check for more things to pack.And,as for Shivam, he just didn't cared about the world. He was sitting on the sofa watching T.V. I walked to the kitchen where mom was cooking rice. "How much time for dinner?" I asked and was feeling too hungry. "10 mins." replied mom. "OK !" I nodded. My stomach was a bit like growling with hunger.

Still, I waited. finally, mom called us for dinner. I got to the dining table as fast as I could. My eyes were wide open seeing so many different types of dishes. Kofta, jeera rice, tandoori roti, onion salad, papad and along with it, thumbs up.I felt like being in heaven after seeing such a beautiful view of dishes decorated over the table. I instantly understood the reason of it. Mom started to serve the food to everyone and as it reached me, I kinda attacked on it since I wasn't able to control my hunger anymore. It was a great. royal dinner and I really,really enjoyed it a lot.

As I finished eating,I got down the dining table and moved towards the washroom to get myself a facewash. It was around 9:00 PM and I couldn't hear even a pin drop. The only thing I could hear were my own footsteps. I moved on breaking the silence. As I reached to the door of the washovom,I tried. to push open it. It wasn't opening.It Seemed like it was locked from the inside. I felt like shivers blazed throughout my body. As per my memory, everyone seemed to be on the dining table.Who is inside? I thought.I tried to open again but still no progress. It was getting too fishy. One more time, I tried, and this time,with more effort. Suddenly the door opened with a flash. I stepped in to check who was the one inside but, to my surprise, the lights were on but no one seemed to be in there. It felt very anonymous. "Let it be." I said to myself inside.

Getting out of the washroom, then I headed towards the bedroom. It was quiet late and I was also feeling a bit dizzy.Mom n' dad seemed to be in the hall watching T.V. I snuggled in the bed and slept turning off the lights.

The Next Day:

Down the bright city of Nagpur, it was 6:45 AM when more than the half of the city was awake with a beautiful sunrise, the streets of the city started to fill up with the aroma of tasty, delicious snacks being cooked by the street-vendors. Small kids accampamied by old ones got playing on the Raj- garden of Aman Nagar."Triinnggg!!!" Sound I heard of the alarm clock situated on the top left corner of the table beside my bed. I smashed it down with the palm of my hand to stop its ringing sound. Just one day remained for my departure Excitement was at its peak.

I quickly hopped off the bed and ran towards the washroom to brush my teeth. I so excited that I had literally forgotten to have a glimpse of my face which was my daily routine. Getting to the washroom, I did my brushing as fast as I could 'cause I knew that today also there would be something special for breakfast. I hastely reached the dining table and yes, as per my prediction, I could see masala dosa served beautifully along with sambhar.

"This all doesn't seems to be made round here?"I asked to mom throwing some kind of packaging in the dustbin. "Nor it is." replied Mom,"Dad got it from the Gaurav-Restaurant." she continued."The one which has opened recently?" I asked "Yes!Your dad said that it would be great to try its food once."she replied."Yes. Also, I don't think its much time that its built since the demolish of the abbey where today the restaurants stands." I said, "Yup!" she added.

As we were talking, I could see dad entering the kitchen from the backyard door. "Everyone get down the dining table. It won't be good when cold." I could hear him say.What was I waitin' for? I jumped on the dining table, sat down on the chair and slowly started eating enjoying every single bite that melted in my mouth. I could feel from inside that my good luck had started.

It was around 1:00 PM when I was sitting on the sofa couch pondering over a novel named as, "Goosebumps-The Phantom of the Auditorium." I could listen mom talking over the phone. It was more than 10 calls that mom received in a line. The thing that we all were going on the tour just spread like a fire. As I kept on reading, suddenly got a thought about Prashik.Even if the whole world would get to know about our tour, he would be still unaware of everything.

I wanted to call him but to my disappointment, all the phones in the house were kinda busy. "Let it be. I'll try later on." I tried to convence myself. The day then just kept going busy in calls of relatives and neighbours. Our flight was sheduled 11:00 AM the next day while it was evening.Last time, we checked out all of the things we had packed and checked if anything remained. I was glad to find out that nothing was remaining to be packed.

I decided to go out and meet Prashik.I got out and could see many cyclists riding down along the sunset. I strode towards Prashik's home down the street with a hope in my heart that for a last time before departure, I'll be able to meet him. As I reached there, to my disappointment, the door of his house was still locked.With a disappointed heart, I headed towards home while suddenly I heard someone calling for me, "Hey Aditya!" I turned back. To my surprise. I couldn't see anyone. It was abberent.I got back home at around 7:00PM. I was feeling very tired and dizzy. "Mom,I'm going to sleep!" I informed. "What about dinner ?" mom asked. "Let it be for now." I replied walking towards the bedroom. I snuggled inside the bed and just in a few minutes, I slept.

4

Let's Go!

Finally!The day arrived, 8th of March, 2022.My eyes opened at their earliest. Still I could see mom n' dad sitting in the hall,having a sip of tea. I stood up. I was feeling really,really very excited. I raised my eyes. towards the clock hanged on the wall in front of me. I could see the time visible in it, as, 6:30 AM.4 and a half hours were left.We had to leave for the airport in less than 2 hour. I needed to get ready as fast as I could.

I walked towards mom but as soon as she saw me, she said, "Aditya, you woke up? Ok, go and start getting ready. We'll need to leave for airport in around 2 hours", "OK!" I replied and got myself to the washroom.I brushed my teeth and got myself a warm bath and got out of the washroom, turning off the lights.As I walked through the corridor,I felt that lights of the washroom were still on. It seemed awkward. I turned a back, walked towards the door and as I was going to push open it, I was able to see light coming out through a narrow gap on the boundary. As the door opened, I was really shocked to see the darkness inside. Now it was to really-really very abberent.

I got to my room and got adorated with the best outfit I was available with. It was 8:00 AM in the clock while everyone seemed to have got ready to get departed.We waited for our taxi to arrive which would have dropped us at the airport. "Got all your things?"asked mom to me and Shivam. "Yes!" we nodded in reply while suddenly I realised that I had forgot my sunscream which I had specially bought for our trip.

I ran towards my room and flash opened the door. I rummaged around through the bed, table, cupboard but couldn't find the cream while suddenly remembered that I had kept it on the table next to the entrance door. As just as I remembered,I heard a horn of a taxi, which was the same one in which I had to go. "Aditya! Come fast!" I could hear dad calling out for me. I hurried towards the door while my sixth sense told me that something or someone was having an eye over me.

But,I didn't paid much attention and hurried out.I picked up the sunscream,locked the door and hurried to the taxi in which mom,dad and Shivam had already settled.As I reached for the door,mom said,"Get in fast!We need to depart quick!."

I opened the door,got in and sat down comforatbly while the taxi started with a jerk.Finally!We got on our way to Hawai.We rode down the roads of Nagpur to the airport.It was around 8:30 AM when we entered the airport with a slight fainted smile suffused all over our faces.We got our boarding passes and marched towards the waiting area.It was around 9:30 AM then."Lets have a look on its store." I suggested dad and he appreciated the idea.

We walked down exploring the streets of the shops. As we kept on, we reached the section of food where my eyes were wide open to see so many types of snacks and even beverages. I was wondered to see so many sorts of ready-made snacks like poha,noodles,pani puri and even pav bhaji.We went further crossing many sections such as cosmetics, books, decorative items,etc.After seeing so much items, our hearts were fulfilled with satisfaction. We also bought a few things such as a perfume,pendat, facewash, etc.

We got ourselves towards the waiting area while suddenly many people around us started running back and fourth and they gathered near an another person.I went closer to inspect what happened. As I got to it, I could see a person laid down on the floor. "Jeet!!!!!" screamed a person from the crowd. It seemed to be a case of cardiac arrest. "Call for an ambulance quick!" said the man. Just then, another man started to dial 1-0-2 on his phone and called for an ambulance. I could hear him say over his phone in hurry accompanied with worry. "He-Hello ? I-I am Provesh and I-I am talking fr-from the airport. Here a man has got a heart heart attack.Plese come fast!" and he kept down his phone.In a few minutes, an ambulance came making noise by its Siren. We just kept on watching a few people come out of the ambulance holding a stretcher in their hands. They got towards the man lying down named Jeet, and laid him down on the stretcher and carried him to the ambulance.They got him inside while we all could just see everything happen.

"Himanshu,you should go along with Jeet. I'll handle everything here." Said the man who the called for the ambulance. "OK." said the other man named Himanshu and walked towards the ambulance and got in.Just then, the ambulance started taking away both of them.

"Wasn't that too fast?" I said to mom."Yes, I hope the man gets well." replied Mom while suddenly we got to know that our flight had landed. We headed towards our plane and you can guess my excitment by the incident that I bumped my head into a glass pane in there while entering inside the plane. Still, I somehow managed myself to get in along with a trolley in my hand. I entered inside and could see many people arranging their luggage in their seats. I followed dad to our seat and I was literally amazed to see we got a window seat.

I settled down beside the window through which I could see a few planes and the runway. I got my hand inside a bag,and took out a packet of chips while an air hostess came in front of us all and started to give instructions, she told about the doors, seatbelts and safely-items. After she finished, we were instructed to switch-off our phones. And everyone, one by one started to switch off their phones while I enjoyed eating my chips.

As I kept a chip in my mouth, I heard two people talking behind me, "Prathamesh, do you remember that about an hour ago, a man was taken to the hospital from here?" said one of them to the other."Yes, I do remember. So what Krupesh?" replied the other."I knew that you won't be knowing. He was Jeet, a well known diamond merchant." said the man. "Really?" he replied but I wasn't able to hear anymore.

The plane had started to move slowly towards the runway making very loud noise. It started from slow to very fast.I was seeing the ground moving backward and suddenly the ground started to thrash down, but the thing was that we were in air.We moved higher in the air and really it was a pleasant experience.Now, we had to first go to Kolkata then to Dubai, then.... Hawai.It was a very-very long journey. As for my seat, it was very comfortable along with a screen in my front and a beautiful view on my left.

The time seemed to be going at the speed of light when we were about to land in Kolkata.We were about to reach but Shivam was still sleeping.I gave him a jerk to wake him up.He slowly woke up and started feeling dizzy while evryone felt a shock as the plane had started to land.Rapidly,the plane shooted to the runway and landed down very carefully. Slowly,it ran over the runway to the kinda parking area.Finally,the plane stopped and everyone started moving and we too.

5

On Our Way

Entering the Kolkata airport,we moved to pick-up our luggage.Their were two hours remaining for our plane to depart for Dubai, then a 4 hours wait and then straight to Hawaii.We had to somehow spend our 2 hours,but since it wasn't much time, we just decided to explore the airport.We all started exploring every single corridor of the airport.

As we kept walking, suddenly, I felt something in my body. "I think I need to go to washroom." I informed mom "Return in less than 5 minutes." she ordered and continued, "We'll be wainting here." I walked in the search of washroom but wasn't able to find it. I had to control. I saw a man and shyly asked him kindly."Sir, can you please guide me with the way of the washroom round here, please!" ,"Ok-ok, go near that shop and turn left. You'll locate the washroom their." he replied pointing towards a shop. "Thank you kind sir." I replied him cheesely and marched through the path he guided me.

Finally, I located the washroom and moved in. Literally, I was just about to lose my control. I hurried in but..... to my surprise, all of the washoooms were engaged. Now I was getting very raged. I angrily knocked one of the door and said, "Come out fast!" I didn't get any reply. I knocked again and moved towards a basin stamping my feet. I gazed at my own face in the mirror to make some control.

I was getting more conjusted seeing my uncomfortable face. I turned back and felt like goosebumps all over my body as I saw the door which I knocked was open. I didn't heard anyone or even saw anyone's reflection in the mirror going out. Still, I ignored as I didn't had much.time. I quickly slipped in the toilet, closed the door and did my work fast.

I came out and hurried back to there where mom was waiting for me.Everyone was still standing there waiting for me."I'm back!" I said."Ok!" replied mom and we continued our exploration.It was around 6:00 PM and we had to depart for Dubai quick.We headed towards our plane with our luggage.We got in the plane got our seats and the same process repeated,as before.

After around 10 mins,we were in air flying right to Dubai.Just all as the journey needed to be, it all went so till finally we reached Dubai.Landing on the runway the same way but this time,the outer view was very very different.We got off the plane and now planned that how we would spend our 4 hours.First-of-all,we got out of the airport, got a taxi and rode straight to the world's highest skyscraper, Burj Khalifa. Just before reaching to it properly, I was able to get its clear view through the window. I just wondered the thing that how it was just built up! Crossing the highway, finally we reached our destination.

As we got off the taxi,we all raised our eyes above admiring the beauty and the height of the miraculous skyscraper.We walked through the entrance door and just felt its feel, the smell, the view, the sound was really-really awesome. Their were many people inside, and most of them were tourists. Now, we had to go to the topmost floor cause I knew that reaching their would give me a great-very great landscapic view. As we moved on in the search of an escalator, exploring the corridors of the skyscraper,we saw a LED screen, hanged on a wall which kinda showed the story that how Burj Khalifa was built.

Finally, we reached to an escalator which steadily rose us above to the top-most floor. As we came out, I saw that all the walls were made up of transparant glass panes.A great landscapic view was visible through the glass. Many people were gazing out the window and I too felt an urge to accompany them.It was a very awesome experience.

Then it was around 7 PM when we headed back to the airport for our final flight. Riding a taxi, we soon reached the airport, slowly and slowly we moved towards our plane. Moving through all the narrow corridors, I got inside the plane, located my seat and settled down, for a final time. It seemed dark out the window where I could see many lights flashing very far away.The plane got to the runway and flew above with all of its might. Through the sky and clouds, we were on our final journey and then just, Hawaii! I kept sitting down with all my patience for around an hour.

I checked my watch and the time was around 9:00PM while an air hostess came and asked for dinner. "Do you serve biryani ?" I shyly asked her. "Yes we do. You'll prefer veg or non-veg?" she replied. "Non veg, please!" I answered timidly. She moved on to get other people's order and soon, she came and brought me a plate full of Chicken Biryani. I had it all, full with relish.We were finished with our dinner at around 10:00PM and decided to sleep. I got myself a cushion and slept gaining a comfortable position.

The time passed being in air while suddenly my eyes opened and I saw someone walking through the corridor in front of me. It kinda seemed like mom.I turned my headand saw that mom's seat was empty. I got confirmed that it was mom.I got up and tried to check in there.I walked to their and asked," Mom? Are, you there?" I didn't got any kind of response. I tried asking again but still couldn't hear anything while suddenly I felt a jerk,I used my hand and got support of a wall to stand.Soon, all things started to shake vigoursly. It was making very load noise. Before I could understand anything, I felt another jerk and this time, with more effort and my head strongly bumped in into a wall. And......I.......fainted.

6

Anyone's There?

Dizzily, I woke up while my head was still rolling.I wasn't able to understand anything nor able to see anything as my vision was fainted. But not for long, in just a few seconds, gradually I started getting a clear view but, to my horror,I was lying on the ground with some bushes and branches of a tree, above my head.I felt many, wounds and bruises all over my body. I tried to predict what must have happened. I stood up. I tried but I couldn't see any traces of the plane. I really wasn't able to understand anything. "What should I do now? What has this happened?"I said to myself while tears dropped through my eyes. I really couldn't figure out anything. I got down my knees. It felt like, in just a fraction of second,my life was totally wrecked.

"What will happen now? What if I will never be able to find my my family?" such thoughts... flashed all over my mind.But, I didn't had any chance to give up. I had to somehow toy finding the others. There was no any other option.I stood up, with some hope and determination in heart. Even if I was determined, I somewhere lacked the guidance and a better start that I needed. Still, I manged to start my adventure.First of all, I had to do something for my wounds,then had to secure something for eating. I wiped off my tears and started. walking in the direction I felt suitable. I could see many different types of trees which surrounded me, as I kept walking further.

"It would have better if I got any kind of antiseptic plant for my bruises."I thought. I was not knowing that where I was. Just I knew that it was a kind of forest, but where, I didn't knew. I walked on exploring the forest in the search of something useful. After some time of walking, I reached to a beach. It was full of sand and as long as my eyes fell, the only thing visible was water.

Seeing such a view,a quick thought came in my mind that the land I was standing on, was none the other than an island. As far as my eyes went, the only thing visible till the horizon was just blue, water. I had to just some how survive, but I couldn't drink that my sea water. I turned my head aback and as I had expected, the beach was fully covered with tall coconut trees. I knew that I with could get food and water from the coconuts the tree had.

I got closer to a tree, but I was aware that my fate wasn't in the right direction. The coconuts weren't much ripined and adding more pain to it, they were placed very high above my head. I knew, even if I tried, there wasn't any way to get those coconuts. I had to find something different.Along with a heavy heart and a hungry stomach, I decided to strode along the depth of the forest. I started my expendition without knowing that how long it would last. I walked along with my heart full of worries. I didn't knew that till what extent I was alone.

The day passed as I kept exploring.The sun was setting while I had got myself some berries for eating after toiling hard the whole day.Now, as the sun was setting, I had to get myself a shelter to spend a night in. I tried to search for some twigs and branches so that I could build a shelter for myself but to my disappointment, it was getting darker and darker and I wasn't remaining with time to build a shelter. "What should I do now?" I whispered to myself.

"Rather than building a shelter, better use a ready-made one." I continued as my eyes befell over a kinda short tree, easy enough to climb on.Somehow, I managed to climb up on it and got myself a comfortable position. I slipped my right hand inside of my pocket and took out a berry. Taking a small bite of its, I looked up in the sky where many of the stars seemed to be watching me from the above.

I wondered, gazing at them, where must've all of them dissappeared.As I kept on thinking, I felt someone having a keen eye on me from my behind.I turned back, but none was visible.Only trees and trees as far as my eyes went."Anyone's there?" I asked but no response.Then,I slept soundly.

7

Some Sort of Mystery?

The next morning,I woke up, but to my surprise,I wasn't anymore on the tree.I was lying on the ground. I stood up slowly and tried to discover that where I was standing.It wasn't the same familiar place where I was standing a day before.Now this time, it was really, really, really very abberant. I wasn't able to understand that what was really happening with me,"Am I riding a rollercoaster ride?" I wondered while my eyes fell on an old, broken hut,quite large. It in a way attracted me towards it, and I too, did the same.As I went closer and closer, I felt more and more shivers.

As I reached to it, I saw the door was locked, with an very-very old kind of lock.It was rusted a lot and hence I thought that I could break it but, to my amazement, the lock was kind strong. But, I was eagered to look what was in. This time, I tried pushing directly the door. No progress. Then, I started kicking it. Still no progress.Now I was raged.For a last time,I used all of my strength and kicked on the middle-bottom center of the door and yes, this time the door flew open and strongly fell down along with all of its hinges.

As soon as the door slammed down,a lot of dust blew over my face.Fluttering off the dust, I stepped in walking over the door, which a min ago was standing in front of me. As I entered in, it felt like darkness resided in there since years. Nothing was clearly visible but still I managed to check off some things. Despite being a weak hut, it was quite large.All the walls were dusty and corners full of cob-webs. The room was having lots of furniture such some chairs, a cupboard, a table, 3-4 different doors which may lead to other rooms.

I opened the drawers of the table. Almost all of them were empty except one of them. The last drawer contained a few things such as a photo album, a diary, a few very old kind of wooden toys, and also some other things which I wasn't able to understand what were they.

I picked up the photo album, and turned the first page. It had a name written on it but it wasn't properly visible. Then, I turned another page, and another, and another. There were many photos but, none of them was visible. I tried to blew the dust over it but still they were blur. As I moved my eyes, I located a kind of trapdoor near there. Holding the album in my hand, I walked near the trapdoor. I felt like there was something mystical beneath it.

I bent down and tried to open it......Strongly I fell down and my eyes opened in shock,waking me up. "No! It can't be a dream again!" I screamed as I saw myself lying down.I fell from the tree I was sleeping on. Now, I had fell down from the above, I was hurted a bit. All that was just a dream. The hut, the furniture, the trapdoor and those photos.

"Let it be." I said and planned what to do next.I didn't had any kind of toothpaste or toothbrush so I had to simply clean my mouth with just water.I checked my pockets and got to know that only a few berries were remaining. I had to got for food and find some water too.

I started my expendition and walked past many large trees. Luckily, just after around 10 mins, I discovered short stream of water surrounded by same bushes having the same berries that I was eating. I bent down and cleaned my throat with the water. Pouring out some water in a cup-like structure made by my palms, I gulped a lot of water.Finishing with it, I then started to pluck out some of the berries from the plant, which would help me out to fight with hunger.

About 1-1.5 hour later I found myself on the beach. I was thinking to build a small tent for myself. I was also running short of food but was just thinking that fishes would be great to eat. I turned my head round the beaching in search of some tool for fishing. And yes I was lucky enough to find myself a fishing rod-shaped piece of wood. It was about 15 metres distant from me.I stood up and slowly walked towards it. As I got nearer to it, some kind of miscalleneous sounds vibrated in my ears.Following the sounds, my head turned towards the depth of the fosest. Deep in the dense forest some sort of thing seemed shining. While the sound kept on vibrating.The sound seemed to attract me towards it. I stepped ahead but stopped.

"Should I go ahead, or not?" I thought. I turned back, but, curiosity kept blazing throughout my body. I tried to stop myself but I couldn't. My body turned by itself and started walking in the direction of the origin of the sound.To my surprise, there was the same hut which I saw in my dream.The same location, the same,the same door and even the same lock.

At this point, I realised that I was kinda building up a sixth sense, a sense where I dreamt of something which was going to happen.Their was something, a secret, a mystery, which I had to find out. Now, I knew that what I had to do. I opened the door the same way I opened it in my dream. The same room, the same furniture and even the same drawer. I felt like a new energy in me. It was all same way in my dream. I got to the drawer and opened it but, in this situation, all the drawers contained some or the other thing .One drawer had some pins and very old rope. The second drawer seemed to contain same sort of wooden structure which was out of my mind. And the last drawer consisted of an old-dusty diary, and an old photo album. I picked up the diary and was just going to open it while my eyes fell over the trapdoor.

I was aware of it.Along with both the books, I walked towards it and opened it. It consisted of ladders going deep down. As per fate's grace, I went down. Down n' down n' down it went,until I hitted ground. It was just one way.

I decided to discover further.In the search of a new hope, I started walking.In there,all the torches seemed very old but still they were burning without any pause. "How!" I asked myself while suddenly I realised that someone was observing me. I turned aback quickly and screamed,"Who is there?" but no reply came, only what I could hear was my echo.I continued walking in the same direction. It totally took me approximately 20 mins to reach its end,where I could find myself at a place from where a lot of light was coming towards me. I ran towards it with all of my strength.

As I got out,my eyes couldn't bear the sudden beam of light falling on them so they closed tight. I slowly opened them and found myself on kind of beach with lots of sand and the sea in front of me. I saw something shining in front of me and walked towards it. It seemed to be some sort of pearl. I ignored it and turned to go around while I saw some bushes shaking at a short distance.Now I had enough,

I had to find out who was behind me.I held my breath and ran towards it with all of my strength,cleared the bushes. My eyes were wide n' wide open in shock to see someone familiar one standing in front of me.

8

Aaaaaaahhhhhh!!!!

"Prashik!How did you came up here?" I asked in shock. "I-I don't know. You know, I came to a free tour, with my parents, but don't know how I saw myself here.What I could remember was that I had slept in the plane while I felt a kind of jerk and when I woke up, I found myself lying down here. I can't tell you how happy I am to see you here. But, how did 'you' came here?" he finished. "The same as you. But, I don't know what to do next. We need to find our families", "I said.

"You're correct, but do you have any plan?" he asked. "Just keep walking." I said. We started walking in a random direction with some hope in our hearts. As we were walking, I kept on my talking to him to soothen my mind. I was happy too, to find someone and I was not lonely anymore. As we seemed to be in the middle of the forest, the sky dusked and shadows got long and hard. "It's better to get a shelter and have a nice sleep." I suggested.

"Nice idea." He agreed and started looking for some branches nearby to make kind of a cute shelter. After toiling for around 20 mins, finally we created a small shelter and a fireplace. The berries we had got on way was our dinner.We had some of them with relish till it was late night and then, we slept.

Even being fast asleep,I could hear some sort of anonymous sounds which woke me up. I woke up but couldn't see anything since the fire was burned out. "Pratik ?" I called for him but... he didn't seemed to be there "Prashik?" I asked for him once more no reply but the sound increased. I was starting to feel a bit scared. Suddenly J could hear a woman screaming. It was getting very horrific.

I was able to feel my heart beat on every single part of my body.I couldn't express my fear. It getting more and more every second.I came out in the woods. I felt like I was gathered by many people. The echoe, woman crying, and the sobbing of a child was all I was hearing.

From my behind,I heard someone calling for me.I turned aback but...... my eyes blurred,heart freezed, blood ran cold what not happened seeing such a thing in front me. It had-had a totally broken face. Blood blanketing it completely, and one eye popped out, big deep scratch marks on its body. It was very fearful. I screamed and started to run in the opposite direction.... "Haah!Haah! Haah!" I wheezed while I ran holding my breath.I ran to my my life until I reached a kind of cave where a I felt comfortable. It all stopped. I turned aback to see if it was still there.

But, I could still see someone running towards me but I was pleased to see it was was Prashik."What was it? And where were you?"I asked him assuming that he also saw the same as me." I-I don't know. I had just got out for washroom"he said.We tried to find what place we were standingIt seemed like a cave. We walked and reached the exit of it. We couldn't figure out what was happening. But, whatever it was, it was very horrific.

It was still night outside.We had to somehow get out of the island.We tried to find, while I heard very loud sound and air coming from upside. I looked above and saw a.......

9

2 Days Later

I wake up in the morning. The sun was blazing out there. I walked a few steps,got hold of a thing and read, 10 people, named Nayan,Bhargav, Harshal, Atharva, Aniket, Lankesh,Rohan,Lokesh,Prashik and Aditya are rescued from aa island near Hawaii. Due to failure in plane, the Pilots named Prajwal, Rohit and 'Jeet' did emergency landing on the island. Many were saved and taken to The Queens Medical Center, in Honolulu, Hawali,The others were shattered but rescued.

"Knock-knock" the door knocked."Come in, its open" I said. It was Prashik. "Why did you call me here?" he asked. "I want to show you something"I said and took out the photo album and diary I found in the hut." "What are these ?" he asked. "Just something I wanna know," I replied.

First, I opened the diary while Prashik said, "You continue,I'll come from washroom." ,"OK!" I said and started reading the first page,

"No laila, ʻo koʻu lā mua kēia aʻu e kākau nei i kahi diary....."

"Ohh I need to translate it first!" I said to myself and picked up the phone.I translated the page which kinda told the story of a boy living on that island. Maybe it was his hut. I tried to open its last page which read as

"Today, I can't tell you how depressed I am. My father is killed by a tiger.By the shock, my mom also commited suicide. Now I don't have anything to live for.Now, I will also have to hang myself because I can't live anymore."

I read it and the date read as 19th May 1957. I hastely opened the album to see the photos. Luckily I found the photo of the child. He was Prashik.

From The Author

Thanks for reading it and I am sorry for any mistakes in it.I know it can't be perfect but I'll try to improve by time.Hope you enjoyed it and Thanks once again.

Printed by Libri Plureos GmbH in Hamburg,
Germany